Bamboo, Velvet and Beak

The Furry Caterpillar

Felicia Law

Illustrated by Claire Philpott

Coloured by Xact Studio

allegra

Bamboo, Velvet and Beak wake up
on their log in the rainforest,
just as they always do...

'Have you seen my egg?' asks Beak.
'I put it on the log ready to eat
for breakfast.'

4

'No,' says Bamboo.
'No,' says Velvet.
'What's under your head then?'
asks Beak.

'It's my pillow,' says Bamboo.
'My furry pillow.'

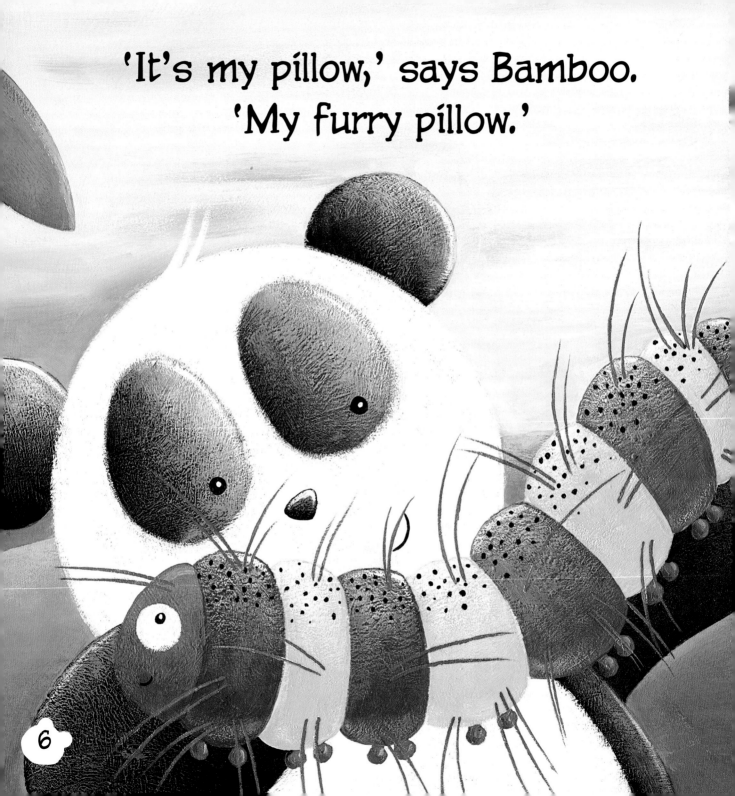

'It's not your furry pillow,' says Beak.
'It's MY furry caterpillar. It hatched
out of MY egg, so it's MY breakfast.'
'It's not,' says Bamboo.
'It's MY pillow.'

'Pillows don't hatch from eggs,'
says Bamboo. 'And you can't eat it.
Its soft and tickly. And it's mine'.

'It's not!' says Beak.
'It is!' says Bamboo.

'Your pillow seems to be very hungry,' says Velvet. 'It's eating a lot of leaves.'

10

Velvet is right. The pillow eats and
eats. And it gets fatter and fatter... 11

...until it splits!

12

'Oops!' say
Bamboo, Velvet and Beak.

13

An even larger furry caterpillar
slides out of the split skin.

'Hey, MY pillow's even bigger,'
says Bamboo.
'So is MY breakfast,' says Beak.

15

Every day the caterpillar eats and eats.
Every day its skin splits and an even
larger caterpillar crawls out.

'Lovely pillow,' says Bamboo.
'Lovely breakfast,' says Beak.
'Stop arguing!' says Velvet.

Then one day the argument ends.
Bamboo wakes up to find a kind of
hard shell under his head.
'Where's my furry pillow?' he says.

'It's hiding in that shell,' says Velvet.
'It's hiding from both of you. It's sick
of your quarrelling - just like I am.' 19

'I don't want a hard pillow,'
says Bamboo. 'You can have it, Beak.'
Beak taps the shell.
'It's a bit tough,' he says.

'All shells are tough,' says Velvet,
'but it may be soft in the middle.'

'Crack! Crack! goes the shell,
and it splits apart.
Out flies a beautiful butterfly!

'Goodbye,' it says. 'I'm off to lay an egg.'

'Oh no!' says Velvet. 'Not another egg! The argument's going to start all over again!'

23

The stories in the 'Bamboo, Velvet and Beak' series
find the three animals sitting together, observing
the rainforest and the events that come
and go around them.

Other titles in the series:
The Daddy-long-legs; The Rainbow;
The Feathers; The Walk;
The Tree; The Lunch; The Flower;
The Creeper; The Bird.